GWINNA

GWINNA

STORY AND PAINTINGS BY

BARBARA HELEN BERGER

PHILOMEL BOOKS   NEW YORK

I wish to thank you, Patricia and Nanette, with all my heart.
Special thanks go also to the harpers—Duncan, Silé, Karen,
Dusty Strings, Kim, Therese, James and Jan.
I am grateful too for the trees who were the source of paper for this book.
A portion of the proceeds will be given to forest replanting projects,
to help replace them. —BHB

Published by Philomel Books,
a division of The Putnam & Grosset Group,
200 Madison Avenue, New York, NY 10016.
Printed in Singapore.
Typography by Nanette Stevenson. Calligraphy by Jeanyee Wong.
The text is set in Garamond #3.

Library of Congress Cataloging-in-Publication Data. Berger, Barbara Helen
Gwinna / Barbara Helen Berger. p.   cm. Summary: Having grown a pair of wings
and felt the longing for the freedom of the skies, twelve-year-old Gwinna goes to
the Mother of the Owls, who sends her on a quest to find the songs of the wind.
ISBN 0-399-21738-X [1. Fantasy.]   I. Title. PZ7.B4513Gw 1990
[Fic]—dc19 88-30676 CIP AC
10 9 8 7 6 5 4 3

To Jerry

Contents

GWINNA

There was a girl named Gwinna. This is her tale, as true as I know, true as I heard in the wind. If ever you have been to that land, you may know of Gwinna. For the people there remember her songs. They love to tell of the times she came to them. They'll show you a feather she left behind. Or they'll show you a place where they saw her in the forest, or in the sky. They say you need only to ask the owls and they will send for her. But let me go to the very beginning of Gwinna's tale. It begins before she was born.

I

The Feather

Long ago, in a land of hills and valleys, there was a man and his wife. They lived on a hillside, with the sky above, and the village in the green valley below.

The man was a woodworker. He made their house and everything in it: the table, the chairs and the bed. He made a cradle too, for the child they longed to have for their own. Yet moon after moon, summer, fall, winter and spring, the cradle was empty. No child came.

At last the woman said, "Let us go to the Mother of the Owls and ask for her help."

Now some in the village said the Mother of the Owls was an evil witch. Others said she was wise. The man asked his wife, "How can we know?" And she said to him, "One or the other, wicked or wise, she will have the magic we need."

So telling no one where they were going, the man and his wife went out the gate and down the road, down through the

valley, and deep into the forest. No one from the village saw them go.

The forest was dim with mist. It wove in and out of tall columns of trees, in and out of tangled branches. Even in day it was dim as dusk, neither light nor dark. "It is owl-light," whispered the man. The woman nodded. Yet if any owl flew in the mist, they did not hear it, for an owl's wings are silent. Nor did they hear any owl's voice, till they came to a wall of great gray stone, hung with a curtain of ivy.

The ivy covered an opening in the stone. A voice called out from within, "Huuuu. Huuuu."

The man stood where he was. "This is a woman's business," he said. He squeezed the hand of his wife to give her courage. But it was her longing for a child that made her brave. "I will speak for both of us," she said. Then she parted the ivy curtain, and it rustled closed again behind her.

She found herself in a large grotto. The darkness smelled of rotting leaves, pungent and sweet. Somewhere, water trickled out of the stone. The roof was open. And through the lacework of branches above, the dim light of the forest filtered down.

"Huuuu," said the voice again.

There was an old crone, sitting in a pool of silver light. She wore a great shawl of feathers. Her hair was spun of cobwebs and mist, catching the twigs and leaves she wore like an untidy crown. And though her face was dark with wrinkles, her eyes shone out like two full moons, midnight each in the center.

"Huuuu," said the old crone once more. "Why do you come?"

The woman made a deep curtsy. "Mother of the Owls," she said, "I come for a child of my own. Will you help me?"

Slowly, the old woman spread her arms to either side, parting her shawl like the wings of a great mother bird. "See," she said, "I have many children."

Within the shawl, the woman saw many animals. There were foxes, rabbits and deer. There was a wolf and a bear. There were owls of course, of every kind, and many other birds. They all flew out from under the shawl, twittering, chirping and hooting. The other animals too came out from beneath the shawl. The wolf and the bear sniffed at the woman as they passed, then they settled quietly with the others, all around the grotto.

"Even the stones are my children," said the Mother of the Owls. "If you wish to have a child of mine, you must give me a promise in return."

Trembling, the woman said, "I will give anything."

"Well then," said the Mother of the Owls. "As above, so it shall be below."

She stood, and pulling a feather from her shawl, she held it high over her head. The feather seemed to gather a light into itself. Slowly, the old woman pulled it down, and bending over, she touched the glowing tip of the feather to the ground. Then she swept something up from the earth and cradled it in her arms. The woman saw nothing there. But the Mother of the Owls held it, gently rocking back and forth, touching it with the feather, crooning softly in words the woman did not understand.

Then the Mother of the Owls lifted what the woman could not see. And just as if it were a bird, she let it go. But the glowing feather was still in her hand.

She held the feather out to the woman and said, "You will have a girl child. She will be like no other. But do not be afraid. Keep this feather always over her bed, for it is my blessing." There were twelve stripes on the feather, silver and white. "In this many years, I will send for my child. And then you must let her go."

The woman took the feather, and pressing it to her heart, she said, "I promise."

Ribbons

Hand in hand, the man and his wife went back through the forest with light, hopeful steps. And sure as winter turns to spring, when they came home, they found a baby lying asleep in the cradle.

What a lovely baby she was. The hair on her head was a coppery fuzz. Her tiny ears were perfect. When she opened her eyes, they were pale green and clear as water. She was a fine baby in every way, but for two dark spots upon her back, just below the shoulders.

"They are only birthmarks," said the man.

The woman held the baby close to her and wept for joy. Then they hung the feather over the cradle. And they called the baby Gwinna.

Gwinna was a happy child. Soon she was taller than her papa's knee. He carved little wooden toys for her. And often, when she played in the grass, the sparrows fluttered around her. Gwinna ran after them, reaching out to catch their songs out of the air with her fingers. Her laughter seemed to fly up and tumble down the hillside, like small bells ringing.

At night, even when there was no moon, the feather glowed over Gwinna's bed. And all was peaceful in the house, and in the valley below.

But as Gwinna grew, so did the two dark spots. Her mother worried. She rubbed the spots with healing balms. But soon they grew into nubs. She tried every remedy she knew. Still the nubs grew until one day, Gwinna's mother saw the start of two small wings. They were covered with soft gray down. But Gwinna's mother felt no joy to see them. She was afraid. She ran to her husband and they worried together.

"What if she tries to fly? We can never teach her."

"She will fall. She will be hurt."

"And if she flies away?"

"Then she will be lost!"

Gwinna's mother tore a snow-white cloth into ribbons. Then she wound them round and around, binding the downy winglets close to Gwinna's back. "Ribbons, ribbons, snow-white ribbons, keep my Gwinna safe," she said.

No one in the village noticed the slight hump in Gwinna's back, under her dress. The coppery curls of her hair fell over her shoulders. Even so, the people would not have noticed, they were so taken with Gwinna's face.

"Even when she does not smile, she glows," they said.

"And when she laughs, she sings."

The village children loved to play with Gwinna. They ran with her in their bare feet, for Gwinna said, "Let's never wear shoes." They sat with her on the hillside naming the shapes of the clouds.

"Look, a haycart."

"No it's a cow."

"A lion. A griffin. A goose!" They made silly tunes together. And then the children ran home to the village, flowers from the hillside woven in their hair.

"Mama, look," Gwinna said, holding out her skirt like a basket, full of wildflowers.

"I see your dirty feet," her mother said. "But I am glad to know they are safe on the ground." Gwinna looked at her feet and wondered where else they could be. Her mother only kissed her and put the flowers in a bowl on the table.

Oh how Gwinna's mother hoped the ribbons would keep the wings from growing. But as Gwinna grew, so did the hump in her back. Then one day when Gwinna's mother unwound the ribbons to change them, she saw the soft gray down was gone. There were new feathers, the colors of the earth. They were matted and dark as leafmold.

"Oh my poor unlucky child!" her mother cried.

"What is wrong, Mama?" Gwinna asked.

"Do not look, my girl," her mother said to her. "There is nothing good to see." And she broke the looking glass. "But do not be afraid, I will keep you safe. And the wind shall never take you."

She tore a fresh cloth into ribbons. Then she wound them round and round, crissing, crossing, front and back, under and over and all around, binding the wings to Gwinna's back, over her petticoat.

"Mama, it hurts," said Gwinna.

"It is only the ribbons, snow-white ribbons, to keep my Gwinna safe," her mother said. Gwinna didn't dare to turn and look, or touch, as her mother tied the ribbons with a great knot. Then she took the feather down from over Gwinna's bed.

Gwinna reached out. "My feather."

"My darling girl," said her mother, "this is not a blessing but a curse. I must use a magic of my own." But she would not let Gwinna see. Alone she went outside the house, and dug a hole in the ground by the well. There she buried the feather. "What was above is now below," she said. And she set a heavy stone over the place.

3

The Wind

From that day, the bells of Gwinna's laughter hardly rang. Her face that glowed was pale. Seasons passed, and still the wings grew under the ribbons. Soon, nothing could hide the hump of her back anymore.

People whispered, "Poor girl."

"She is stiff and bent as a little old crone."

The village children tried to be kind, but they quickly looked away. Gwinna waited, wondering why they never came to play with her anymore. But when she saw the shape of her own shadow, she looked away too.

She climbed the hillside alone. There she sat looking up at the clouds. Yet nothing eased the ache in her heart. And nothing eased the ache in her back, under the ribbons. It is a curse, she thought, Mama was right. "O wind," she sighed, "O wind, what will become of me?"

The wind only ruffled her hair and dried the tears from her

face. No one saw the tears at all, only a sparrow who sat on a branch by her knee, silent. Gwinna said sadly, "Where is your song, little sparrow?"

How strange it was. She was so alone, yet all the land seemed to be sad with her. The spring was slow to come. There were not many wildflowers. The trees were hardly green before the leaves began turning brown. Even the grass was dull under Gwinna's feet. Every day when she went to the well with the bucket, she felt a chill in the ground that did not belong to summer. Soon, too soon, she would have to wear shoes again.

Down in the village, people murmured, "The land is under a curse." No one dared to say the name of the Mother of the Owls. But at dusk, they went out into the streets and beat upon pots and pans, to keep the owls away.

When the clamor came up the hillside, Gwinna's mother shivered and pulled the curtains closed. Then she held Gwinna close, and rocked her gently in her arms before she said goodnight.

Up in her room alone, Gwinna lifted the curtain from her window. She wanted to let the moonlight in. She wanted to see the clouds soaring in silence, under and over the moon. What is it like, she wondered, to fly so high, so quiet and free? When the dark shape of an owl flew past her window without a sound, Gwinna felt a restless tingle under the ribbons. The ache in her shoulders grew so sharp, she gasped. It is only the cold night wind, she thought, though everything was still.

Then one day Gwinna woke at dawn. She unlatched her window. And there, beyond the brown hills, beyond the end of the valley, she saw a mountain. Gwinna held her breath. She had never seen the mountain before, rising alone, high and dazzling white. Though the mountain was far, far away, she could see a light on the icy peak, as if a spark from the rising sun came to rest there. Then the light grew and poured down the mountainsides. Gwinna saw it rushing toward her in a wind, blowing over the hills, swirling through the grasses and tossing the tired trees, turning them all to green as it came. She heard the songs of a thousand green summer leaves. Before her, the whole valley shimmered with light and rang with melodies. As Gwinna leaned out her window to hear, the wind rushed up the hillside, brushing the music into her ears as it passed, up over the roof of the house and away.

Then, the green faded again from the trees and the hills. The valley was dull as before. But Gwinna still heard the music, after the wind was gone. She felt it ringing inside her, just as a harp will ring, even after the harper's hands are still.

She pulled on her dress and ran downstairs. Her mother was setting the morning bread on the table. Her father came to sit down.

"Mama, Papa! Did you hear it?" Gwinna's face shone as she tried to sing what she heard. Her own voice was too thin and small. But her father and mother smiled. "Where did you get that pretty tune?" they asked.

"It came in the wind, just now, from the mountain."

"What mountain can that be?" said her father. "There is no mountain here, only the hills."

"But, it is far away," said Gwinna.

"Even on the clearest day, I have never seen a mountain," he said gently. "I think it must have been a cloud you saw."

Gwinna ran to the open door. Clouds were always changing, but the mountain was still there. "See?" she said, pointing.

They did not see it.

Gwinna could hardly eat her bread and butter. Her father turned to his workshed. Her mother turned to the wash. "Come, my dear," she said. "Come out of your lovely dream."

So Gwinna went out to help her mother hang the wash on the line. Again and again, she turned to look at the mountain as she worked. The higher the sun rose in the sky, the brighter the mountain was. At last, when the wind came again, and the trees on the hillside swayed, Gwinna tugged on her mother's sleeve. "Listen, Mama. Do you hear it?"

Her mother stopped a moment. Then she smiled. "I hear

clean wash flapping in the breeze. It is music enough for me."
And she took the washtub back into the house.

True, the aprons, trousers, dresses and sheets were dancing
gaily in the wind. But Gwinna heard something more. All
around her were joyous tunes and leaves of lilting green. With
every breath, the wind filled her with such music and light,
she thought it would sweep her away. She wanted to go. If only
she had wings like the birds, she would. She would fly wherever the wind might carry her, even as far as the sea. Yet when
the wind blew over the hill and was gone, Gwinna's feet were
still on the ground. And the song ringing inside her was so
radiant and big, and Gwinna was so small, she felt as if she
would break into a hundred pieces.

Then Gwinna did see a cloud. The sky was empty a moment
before. Now, she saw a white plume rising over the mountain.
Slowly, the cloud gathered and grew into a graceful shape.
Gwinna whispered its name. "A harp." The cloud was a harp,
great enough for the hands of the wind to play.

"A harp." Gwinna went to the edge of the hill, reaching out
into the air, longing to touch the strings of the harp in the sky.
If only she could play the song of the wind. If only she could
play the music inside her. With a sigh, she let her hands fall,
as the harp of cloud drifted away, and the last bit of green
faded again from the trees.

Then, as if the smallest breeze whispered it into her ear, Gwinna thought, There are harps here below, too. Small harps for people to play. Harps made of wood.

She ran to her father's workshed. There she found him joining a leg to a chair. The floor was covered with shavings. "Papa," Gwinna said. "Papa, please, will you make me a harp?"

Gwinna's father looked up. "A harp?" he said. "To build a harp takes a master's hand." He smiled at Gwinna, a little sadly, and said, "You are young for a harp."

"I am twelve, Papa."

Her father only laid his big hand upon her head. He loved his Gwinna dearly. So he made a stool for her instead.

By suppertime it was done. The stool had a pretty seat, and three carved legs. Gwinna thanked her papa, and sat on her new stool, trying with all her might not to cry. She loved him, and her mama. But they didn't hear the song she heard. They didn't see the mountain. As she sat with them by the fireside, she felt more alone than ever.

Gwinna cried herself to sleep, in her own bed in the dark. With tears sinking into her pillow, she tried to remember the song. Now, she heard only a voice in the trees outside her window. All night long the voice called softly, softly, like a small wooden flute. "Hu, hu, hu. Hu, huu."

4

Owl-Light

A mist shrouded the hills and filled the valley all the next day. The trees seemed to drown in a sea of gray, and the sky was the same. Soon even the nearest rim of the hillside disappeared. Gwinna knew there was no hope of seeing the mountain. She leaned on the kitchen window sill, looking out. Everything was dim as dusk, neither light nor dark.

Her father said, "It is owl-light."

Gwinna's mother began to tremble and shake. The spoon dropped from her hand. She pulled the curtain over the window and said to her husband, "Bolt the door." He did as she said, pulling the bolt shut with a loud thud.

"Gwinna," said her mother, "my child, don't be afraid. We will never let you go."

Before Gwinna could ask her, "Where?", there were hoots and screeches and calls outside the house.

"Do not listen!" said her mother. "Do not look!" said her

father. "Be as still as a stone." They pressed their hands over their ears and shut their eyes. But Gwinna heard the sounds.

"Whoooo. Hoo-OOOO. Skireeekh, tu-whoooo!"

She wanted to see. Slowly, she lifted the curtain and peeked outside. An owl swooped near the window. Then another. One by one, owls appeared out of the mist and vanished again, circling the house. Some were large, others smaller. One was snowy white. They flew by the window on silent wings, looking in at Gwinna. When she looked back into their eyes, she found she could understand them.

"Gwinna," called the owls. "Hooo, tu-whooo. We have come for you."

"Mama, Papa," Gwinna said, "how do the owls know my name?"

But her mother and father kept their eyes shut and their hands over their ears. They were still as two statues, a man standing and a woman in her chair. Gwinna went to touch them, but they did not seem to feel her hand. Her father's sleeve was strangely cold. Not a fine hair stirred on her mother's head. "Mama? Papa!" Gwinna tried to pull their hands from their ears. She could not move them. Then, she saw a shadow passing over their faces, gray as stone.

Outside the window, outside the door, the owls called, "Tu-whooo, Gwinna, HOOOO. Come with us!" But Gwinna sank down on her stool in horror. Then she jumped up. The stool was wood no more, but cold stone. The table too, even the bread on the table. The fire flickered out in the hearth, and the air in the house grew heavy. Gwinna's heart sank in her chest. "I will be stone too."

"Hoo-OOO!" called the owls. "Come out, come with us!"

Gwinna tried to move. Her feet were heavy. She cried to the statues, "Mama, Papa, I must go. Before it is too late!" She saw the gray creeping across the floor like a shadow, toward the walls and the door. A door of stone would be too heavy to open. Quickly, Gwinna laced up her shoes, and put on her hooded cloak. Then she ran to the door and pulled the bolt free. As soon as the door was half open, cool mist came swirling in, slowly, softly winding around the table and chairs, around the two statues.

"I must go," Gwinna whispered, choking back her tears. "O gray ribbons of mist, keep my mama and papa safe." Then she went out of the house. But she could not close the door behind her. It had turned to stone.

All she could see outside was a patch of ground where she stood. Everything else faded away into gray. Somewhere in the mist ahead, the owls called, "Hoo-ooo, hoo-oooo." There was no other sound. Slowly, Gwinna walked toward the voices. When she came to the gate and opened it, the hinges creaked

as they always did. But beyond the gate, it seemed all the world was lost, and she was stepping into nothing, nowhere.

Gwinna turned, looking back, but the house had vanished too. As she lifted her hand, reaching into the mist to somehow say good-bye, a tiny owl appeared and perched on her arm.

His feathers were snowy white, tipped with silver, soft as cloud-feathers all the way to his talons. His feet gripped Gwinna's arm gently above the wrist. He was no taller than her hand. The little owl stared at Gwinna with eyes as bright as two gold moons, midnight in the center. "Little owl," she said to him, "I don't know where to go."

He bobbed his head up and down and hooted, whistling like a small wooden flute. "Hu! Hu!" The other owls answered, in the mist beyond the gate. "Hooo hoo-hoooo. Follow us. We know the way. Hoo-OOOO."

So Gwinna began to walk toward the owls' voices. She was more like a little old crone than ever, in her hooded cloak. The tiny owl stayed on her arm. Every few moments he hooted, and the other owls answered, flying silently ahead. Twigs snapped under Gwinna's feet as she followed. She walked and walked, there was no telling how far, or where, or how long. Every stone she saw in the mist made her think of her mama and papa. "Hu, hu," called the little owl. "Hoo-ooo, hoo-ooo," called the others.

Tangled branches and thorny briers caught at her in the mist. Many a time she tore her cloak free. Many a time her shoes sank in the mud. Many a time she stumbled and fell over logs that loomed in the way. The little owl flapped his wings and balanced again on Gwinna's arm. "Hu, hu, hu!"

"O little owl," Gwinna said, "where are you taking me?" She was muddy and scratched and tired. The damp chill of the mist went through her cloak. The ribbons pinched. And she could not forget the sorrow that weighed in her heart like a stone.

At last, the mist began to thin. Gwinna saw tall columns of trees. She saw a large owl leaving a branch to fly ahead. Then she saw a wall of stone, hung with a curtain of ivy.

One by one, the owls flew toward it, lifting the strands of ivy away with their talons. They sat on branches to either side, holding the ivy curtain apart. And Gwinna saw an opening there in the stone. The little owl turned his head to look at her. He blinked at her once. Then he flew from her arm, into the dark opening.

Gwinna did not follow. The doorway into the stone before her seemed even deeper than night. She heard the flute of the little owl's voice, echoing within. "Hu-hu-u-u." Silly girl, she thought, it is only a cave where you can lie down and rest. So she took a deep breath. And then she went inside.

5

Mother of the Owls

The ivy fell closed behind her. Gwinna came into a large grotto, filled with a soft silver light. The walls were stone, but the roof was open. There were the owls, coming to roost in the dark branches above. Below them an old, old woman sat in the heart of the grotto, robed in a shawl of feathers. The tiny white owl was perched on her arm.

"Huuuu," said the old woman. "Thank you for bringing my little one home to me."

Gwinna said, "He led the way, or I would be lost."

The old crone smiled at her. "You are truthful," she said. Upon her arm, the little owl scratched himself and fluffed his feathers. She lifted him up. "His name is Tobin."

Gwinna stepped closer. In the silver light, she could not be afraid. "Who are you?" she asked the old woman.

"I am Mother of the Owls, and many more. They are all my children, all your brothers and sisters."

"But I have no brothers and sisters," Gwinna said. "I am alone. And now I have left my home." Looking down, she clutched at her cloak to keep from crying. "My . . . my mama and papa have turned to stone."

The Mother of the Owls clucked very softly and sighed. "Gwinna," she said. "I am your Mother before your father and mother. Before you were born, I held you here in my arms. I touched you with the feather of my blessing. I sent you to the cradle. But your mother and father did not keep their promise."

Gwinna looked up into the ancient woman's eyes. She found there a sorrow even greater than her own. The Mother of the Owls sighed again. Her sigh filled the grotto like a weary wind stirring the weary trees.

Gwinna trembled. "What will happen to Mama and Papa? Will I ever see them again?"

"Someday you may," said the old woman. "But now, do not be afraid for them. Even the stones are my children, and nothing can harm them." Then she opened her shawl and said, "Come."

Every feather in the shawl was glowing, silver and white, like the one that once hung over Gwinna's bed. She felt the light of the shawl enfolding her, fresh and peaceful as the light of the moon. Leaning into the old woman's breast, she heard a heart beating there, a deep, quiet drum.

"Mother before my mother," Gwinna whispered, "may I call you Grandmother?" Into her ear, the old woman whispered, "Yes."

Then, from every corner of the grotto, animals appeared. They must have been in the shadows, or deep in burrows and dens. Grandmother said to them, "Here is your sister, Gwinna."

Curious and shy, a deer came closer and gazed at her. A coppery fox came and sniffed. The rabbits stood up to have a look, their noses twitching up and down. They came to nibble the hem of her cloak, and Gwinna bent down to touch the soft fur behind their ears. A bear nudged Gwinna with his head, nearly pushing her over. It was only a greeting. She hugged him and buried her hands in his thick black fur. Then a mother wolf came close, swinging her tail. Her three pups scampered and jumped, yipping and yapping, licking Gwinna's face with their warm tongues.

Gwinna looked around her in wonder. "So many sisters and brothers." There were more, birds who flew down through the roof, chittering and chattering. And there were owls of course. Tobin was flying in circles around her head.

Before long, everyone settled down. Grandmother said,

"Now my dear, take off your cloak and rest. You have come a long way." Looking down at Gwinna's muddy shoes she asked, "Why did you walk?"

"How else could I go, Grandmother?" Gwinna laid her cloak aside.

"You have wings," Grandmother said. "They were my gift to you. But my dear child, how can anyone fly with her wings inside her dress?" She peered at the hump on Gwinna's back. "Let me see."

Gwinna took off the dress and stood in her petticoat. Grandmother frowned. One bony finger touched the ribbons. "What are these?"

"These are the ribbons, snow-white ribbons, to keep me safe," said Gwinna.

Then Grandmother's eyes flashed. Her silver light turned to lightning. Gwinna saw something gleam in the old woman's hand, sharp as a blade. Before she could move, Grandmother took hold of the ribbons. She slipped the blade up under the knot, and said, "Ribbons, ribbons, binding ribbons, set my child free."

An owl screeched. Fast as a lightning stroke, the blade cut through the knot. Then Grandmother pulled the ends of the ribbons, uncrissing, uncrossing, unwinding, unbinding, turning Gwinna this way and that, till she nearly fell down dizzy.

In a daze, she saw Grandmother's hand flinging the ribbons down to the ground. She heard the bear rumbling and growling. He tore at the ribbons with his claws. The fox and the wolf pups ran at them too, snarling and pulling and ripping the ribbons to shreds. Even Tobin swooped down with his sharp talons. Then the rabbits carried the shreds away, until there was nothing left of the snow-white ribbons, nothing at all.

"Huuuu," Grandmother said. Her silver light was calm again and the grotto was quiet. Gwinna swayed on her feet. The ache in her back spread into every part of her.

Grandmother crooned softly, "Huu, h-huuu," as if to a wounded bird. Gently, she pulled one of Gwinna's wings partly open. "See," she said. Gwinna turned, and saw her own wing for the first time. Then Grandmother pulled the other partly open too.

"Wings," Gwinna whispered. "I do have wings. Oh, I never knew." And hot, stinging tears ran down her cheeks.

Gently, gently, Grandmother pulled the wings all the way open. A sharp pain shot through each one like fire. "Ohhh! Ohhh! It hurts," Gwinna cried.

Grandmother nodded, her own eyes filled with tears. "It

means your wings are alive," she said. "They are only crippled and sore." The feathers were matted, twisted and bent, grown all wrong under the ribbons. Even the bones hurt. Gwinna didn't dare to ask if she would ever fly.

"Come," Grandmother said. She led her to a bed of soft, dry heather and moss. "Lay yourself down, while I go and make you a broth."

Gwinna crawled onto the bed, and with a deep sigh, she buried her face in the sweet-smelling moss. Tobin flew to an old root beside her, while Grandmother went to another part of the grotto, and clattered among clay jars and pots. Then the wolf puppies came to the bed and snuggled close to Gwinna. The mother wolf came too, and began to lick her wings. She licked and licked and licked with her patient tongue, to smooth and soften the feathers, to comfort her sister Gwinna.

Gwinna was nearly asleep when Grandmother came with a steaming mug. "Drink this," she said. "It is made from healing roots and leaves." Gwinna raised herself enough to drink the bitter broth, and then sank into the bed again.

As she lay there, she felt Grandmother's two hands on her back, on the place where each wing grew. She felt something flowing from the hands, warm as summer sunshine. The warmth flowed like rivers into her wings, all through the long thin bones, up and down the shaft of every feather. For a long time, Gwinna felt it pouring over her, soaking into her wings like warmest water, until all the pain was washed away.

Grandmother lifted her hands. "Rest now, my child," she said. And so, with the mother wolf on one side, and the pups still nestled close on the other, Gwinna fell sound asleep.

6

Wings

When Gwinna woke there was blue sky in the branches above, and the day-birds were busy. She saw six toads in a row by the bed. One of them blinked. "Good day to you too, little brother," she said, blinking herself. The wolf and her pups were gone. But Tobin was there, asleep on the old root by the bed. He opened one eye and looked at her, then he closed it again.

Gwinna lay under a blanket of feathers. She thought of her bed at home, and her poor mama and papa. Sorrow fluttered awake in her heart like a silent bird. She sat up, and the feathers dragged along with her. Then she remembered. "Wings. My own wings." Gwinna touched the feathers. Now they were soft and sleek and firm, just as they should be. Her own feathers. They glowed with the colors of earth, spotted with lights and dappled with darker shadows. She wondered, Will I really fly?

Grandmother came to the foot of the bed. "It's a fine day," she said, holding up a fresh white petticoat and a new dress. The dress was many colors of brown all woven together. It had two pockets, and big sleeves, and two openings in the back, cleverly made, just right for wings. Gwinna stood up and Grandmother helped her into the petticoat, then the dress. It fit Gwinna perfectly.

"This will keep you warm wherever you go," Grandmother told her. "It is woven of fleeces and furs the animals have given."

"Thank you," Gwinna said. And tucking her hands into the warm pockets she asked, "Where will I be going? Is it cold there?"

The old woman smiled. "Even on a sunny day, it is cold high up in the sky."

Gwinna's heart jumped. Then she would fly! She felt a tingle in her wings, but try as she might she could not raise them. Her wings only sagged to the sides, and the feathers quivered all the way to the longest tips, touching the grotto floor. "They're too heavy," she sighed.

"Piffle," Grandmother said. "No birdling of mine has wings that are too heavy. Yours are only weak. They have never been tried. And a birdling needs to be strong if she is ever going to fly. So come and have your breakfast."

The smell of hot honey porridge came to Gwinna's nose. She was very hungry. So she went to the table, and did what she could with her clumsy wings to sit down without crushing the feathers.

When her bowl was empty, and filled, and empty again, Grandmother brought Gwinna's shoes. All the mud was gone and there were new laces. "Go out to the meadow, yonder," Grandmother said. "There you will find a mossy crag. Many a young bird has flown from there. Watch and see how my children fly. They all have their ways, and so will you. Only be gentle and slow. Your own wings will teach you."

"Will Tobin come?" Gwinna turned to find him, but he was still asleep by the bed. Of course, it was day. All the owls were sleeping. So Gwinna didn't wait another moment. She kissed Grandmother's cheek, and went out through the ivy curtain alone, to find the meadow.

Not a shred of mist was left in the forest. Gwinna soon found her way and came out into a wide, open place. There she saw a rocky crag. The top was high as a house, and covered with a thatch of moss. Gwinna looked for a way to climb up it, but when her hand touched the cold stone she stopped. Maybe a stone can tell what it knows to other stones, she thought. So she whispered into a crevice in the crag, "Mama, Papa, I'm going to learn how to fly." Then she clambered all the way to the top.

Above the brown trees, all around the meadow, the sky seemed to reach up forever, past the highest clouds. There were swallows swooping to and fro, and noisy crows flapping over the trees. Gwinna stood on top of the crag and tried again to raise her wings. How will I ever fly, she thought, if I can't even lift a feather! Below her, the faded meadow grass seemed a long way to fall.

Not knowing what else to do, slowly she opened her arms, reaching wide. And to her surprise, slowly her wings opened too. The feathers reached far past her fingers, to either side. When she lifted her arms, slowly her wings lifted too. And when she lowered them, her wings went down. Every way she moved her arms, her wings followed, until they were too tired to move any more. Gwinna hopped about on the crag in delight, nearly toppling over.

"Caw! Caw!" called the crows. She sat on top of the crag, watching them flap and wheel and glide, the tips of their black wings spread like fingers. When the crows landed down in the meadow they bounced. "Like that! Like that!"

"Like this, like this," chittered the sparrows, flitting from bush to bush. The swallows twittered, "This is the way." They

beat their wings before every loop and swoop and glide.

"So! Like so!" honked the geese. Looking up, Gwinna saw them flying in line, with swift, whistling wingbeats. And high above them all was a hawk, soaring in silent circles. He hardly moved his wings at all. He is riding the air, Gwinna thought.

Just then a hummingbird hovered in front of her face. He was no bigger than Gwinna's thumb and his wings were moving so fast, she couldn't even see them. "Chip, chip," he teased, "try this!" Then he whizzed away and vanished, too fast to see. But a merry sound of bells rang after him. Gwinna was laughing. "I'll never fly like you," she called to the hummingbird. "But someday, maybe I will soar like a hawk."

Day after day, Gwinna came out to the meadow alone and stood on the mossy crag. Every day, while the leaves fell, Gwinna's wings were stronger. Soon she could stretch and raise them high, and move them by themselves, in and out, up and down, keeping her hands in her pockets, while her feathers swept through the air. Her wings were quiet as an owl's, but not yet strong enough to lift her.

Gusts of wind tossed the last leaves from the trees. "Even the leaves can fly," Gwinna said as they whirled over the meadow. "It's the wind that carries them. Will it ever carry me?" Then one day when the wind blew her way, she took a deep breath, and leaped from the crag. For a moment she felt the lift of the air. But her wings were unsure. She faltered and fell to the ground.

There she lay, groaning. "Ohhh, oh, I will never fly." Yet she picked herself up and tried again. Around the meadow she ran and ran, flapping her wings till her shoes hardly touched the dry leaves on the grass. She climbed the crag again and again. Then, in the last light of the day, as the deer stepped into the meadow, and rabbits came out to feed, Gwinna leaped one more time from the crag. Holding her wings steady, feeling the wind in her face, she glided all the way to the end of the meadow, and set her feet down without falling.

"I can do it!" she cried to the trees, the sky and rabbits and deer. By now, her tired wings were drooping. Gwinna had fallen so many times, she limped home to the grotto, breathless and smiling.

There she found Grandmother napping, wrapped in her shawl like a moon fading under the clouds. Tobin was just waking. He flew to Gwinna's arm, his eyes bright as ever.

"Tobin," she whispered. "Soon I can fly out with you at night. Where will we go?" Tobin bobbed his head in circles and whistled, "Hu! Hu!"

Grandmother woke with a weary moan. Every day, though

Gwinna was stronger, the old woman's silver light was a little more dim. Gwinna touched her thin hand. "Grandmother, are you sick?"

Grandmother patted her gently. "I am old," she said. "Older than anyone knows. Soon I will be resting with the stones."

"No, Grandmother," Gwinna said. "I will make you a broth of roots and leaves, and you will be well again."

But Grandmother shook her head. "My birdling girl. All I wish is to see you flying before the winter comes."

A wolf puppy whimpered. Gwinna whispered to Tobin, "I hope I can."

7

The Voice

The very next day, Gwinna felt a trembling all through her wings. She thought to herself, Today I will fly. I can feel it. She stood on the crag, with her wings wide, sweeping them up and down, up and down. All at once, a noisy throng of birds fluttered around her, whistling and chattering.

Gwinna cried out, "Stop teasing me! I will fly today, I know it." She kept her wings moving, up and down, up and down, and she thought the wind she felt was the flurry of all the birds. But it was the sky rushing into her face. Looking down, she saw the mossy crag already far below. When her feet had left it, Gwinna didn't know. She was flying.

"Twittery-chirr-chirrup! She's up! She's up!"

"Caw! Caw! Huzzah! Hurrah!"

Gwinna's own laughter joined the noise, ringing out to the sky and spilling down. But she kept her wits in every stroke of her wings, or she knew she would fall.

Bare treetops spread out below like a deep thicket of

bushes. Taller fir trees pointed up like steeples. Soon Gwinna was higher than small birds can go, and the throng began to scatter. The crows flew off to tell the news to the countryside. And before long, Gwinna was flying alone.

Her wings were strong and quiet. She felt the lift of the air in her feathers. And just as Grandmother said, the higher she flew the colder the blue sky was. The air washed her face like icy water. The flow of it smoothed her dress around her legs.

There below her was more of the world than Gwinna had ever seen. There were billowing hills, and hills huddled together along the valleys. From so high up, the woodlands seemed a soft brown fur over the land. The forest evergreens were dark as shadows. As Gwinna flew, she saw winding silver rivers and streams. She flew over farms and villages. The houses were as small as the wooden toys her papa used to make. A whole flock of sheep was only a cluster of tiny white pebbles. How is the world so big, she wondered, and everything in it is so small!

The hills rolled on and on in waves of violet and blue. Above them, Gwinna found invisible rivers in the air, and hills in the sky, and valleys no one can see. Her wings were sure and easy now. They knew the way. She could skim and turn, climb and dip and glide, as if she'd been flying all her life. And she felt she could fly forever.

Then she came to a great lift in the air. It was so strong rising up, there was no fear of falling. Gwinna simply held her wings open. She let the air carry her up, and up, in wide soaring circles, like a hawk.

Hovering high in the upper air, almost as high as the clouds, Gwinna rested her wings in the light of the sun. Then, she saw the mountain. She smiled, happy to see it again, so alone, so white. The mountain seemed to be floating too, far, far away in a haze of blue. She felt an icy wind in her face. But the wind from the mountain did not sweep her away. It held her wings still. And as before, Gwinna heard the music of green summer leaves, and of strings ringing under the hands of the wind. There was no harp anywhere in the sky. Still, the melodies swept into Gwinna's ears and filled her with joy, from the farthest tips of her wings, to her toes, to her fingers reaching out into the air.

Then, in the midst of the music, Gwinna heard a single voice. A pure, lilting voice, like none she knew. There were no words in the song it sang to her, and Gwinna didn't know why it made her cry. As soon as her tears fell, the wind froze them to bright crystals of ice and blew them away.

By now it was late. The last light of the sun poured down over the mountain. Then the mountain seemed to swallow the sun. The wind was gone. Gwinna tilted her wings, turned and drifted downward as the light went out of the sky, dusk drew over the land below, and it was night.

Suddenly she wondered, Which is the way? She didn't know where she had flown, or how far. Now the land below was dark. But with the joy of the music still in her heart like a flame, Gwinna could not be afraid. She flew on and on through the dark, silent as an owl. Here and there, she heard the clatter of pots and pans in a village below. And then, after a long way, she saw a small white shape flying beside her. "Tobin?"

"Hu! Hu! Hu!" The other owls were with him. "Hoo hoo-hooo. Tu-whoooo. Now you are one of us. H-HOOO."

They all flew on together, Gwinna and the owls, over the dark hills and valleys, over the forest, until they saw a faint silver glow. The owls flew to the trees around that place. Tobin came with Gwinna, gliding down into the pale circle of light. It was Grandmother, standing like a bent-over moon in the meadow. Her ancient face was smiling.

Gwinna set her feet down before her and folded her wings.

Grandmother said, "My birdling girl is more than a birdling now. She has flown."

Tenderly, Gwinna kissed her old wrinkled cheek. "It is you who gave me wings," she said.

There was jubilation in the grotto, far into the night. The animals were merry, even gruff brother bear. All the while,

Tobin sat upon Gwinna's arm, fluffing his feathers and fluting. He was very proud.

But Grandmother's head was nodding as she dozed. "O Grandmother," said Gwinna, "I wish I could give you the music I heard, high up in the sky. I wish you could hear the song that comes from the mountain."

Grandmother blinked, and looked up. "You saw the mountain?"

"Yes," Gwinna said. "And I heard a voice in the wind, a voice of light and leaves, all sweet and green. The song is still ringing in my ears. It came from the mountain. Grandmother, is it the mountain herself who sings?"

Grandmother didn't say. Her old eyes shone with tears. She seemed to see far away. "I have heard it too. Long, long ago, when the world was new. Oh, how long I have hoped to hear that song again."

Gwinna said, "Grandmother, I would play it for you, if only I had a harp. I would play the music all night and all day." Her fingers fluttered in front of her. "See how small my hands are. It wouldn't have to be a very big harp. Oh, what can I do? Where can I go to find a harp of my own? I will give anything!"

"Will you, my dear?" Grandmother asked.

"Yes."

Grandmother laid her own hands over Gwinna's. They weighed no more than two fallen leaves. "Then," she said, "it is time for you to go there."

"Where?" asked Gwinna.

"Where the song begins," said Grandmother softly. "To the mountain."

8

The Mountain

For a day, Gwinna rested her wings, helping Grandmother in the grotto. There were barley cakes to make for the journey. And Gwinna must have warm stockings, and a cap. Grandmother's old fingers were busy with knitting. Gwinna asked her, "What shall I do at the mountain, Grandmother?"

"First, honor the mountain," Grandmother said. "It is very great. Then go to the highest place, and sit, and wait, and listen."

That night, Gwinna slept on the heather bed, the wolf puppies curled up beside her. She woke before dawn and laced up her shoes, tied on her cap, and put the thin barley cakes in her pockets. Then the animals gathered around, to wish their sister well. Gwinna touched every one of them fondly between the ears. "Tobin?" she said. But he was still out. It was not yet day.

Then Grandmother opened her shawl, and Gwinna came into the arms of her fading light. She heard once more the slow, quiet drum of Grandmother's heart. Gwinna whispered, "Will you still be here when I come back?"

Grandmother said, "My child, wherever I am, above or below, I will wait for you. But do not stay away forever." She smiled tenderly. "Now, be on your way. It is a long journey." She tapped Gwinna's head three times, "Huu, huu, huuu." And all at once, Gwinna found herself outside, in the dark and frosty meadow.

She went to the crag and said softly, into the crevice in the stone, "Good-bye, Mama and Papa."

Then she climbed the crag to the top, and there was Tobin, waiting. He flew to her shoulder, his feathers touching her ear. Gwinna still heard Grandmother's heart, drumming faintly all around her. Into the darkness she said, "Grandmother, I will bring the song from the mountain. I promise." And before she raised her wings to fly, she picked up a bit of stone from the top of the mossy crag, and put it into her pocket.

Then without a sound, Gwinna flew up over the bare, black trees. Tobin flew beside her. The other owls too rose up from the forest, filling the dim sky with silent wings. It was good to be flying with them again. Gwinna felt the frosty chill of the air washing her face. She shivered and tucked her hands in her warm sleeves.

Winter is here, she thought as she flew. And the spring never was, nor summer. The first rosy light of dawn began to touch the hills below, but all the land lay dull and weary. Only the rivers and streams had any shine. Soon they would be frozen, white ribbons of ice, binding the valleys.

The owls flew on with her in silence, until the sky grew light. Then they said, "Remember us. H-hooo, tu-w-h-h-o-o-o-o." One by one, the gray, the spotted and horned owls turned on their quiet wings to fly back home. It was nearly day.

Tobin hooted once in Gwinna's ear, a low wavering note. "Oh Tobin," she said, "won't you come with me?" He was flying so near, she felt the wind of his feathers brushing her cheek. His soft wings were not for far flying. "No," she said, "you must go home, I know. Grandmother needs you. But I will miss you, Tobin."

"Hu-u-u-u," he whistled softly. Gwinna felt a pang in her heart to see him turn and fly away. But she flew on, alone once more. And soon she saw the mountain, far off in the morning sky, brighter than any cloud.

On and on she flew, with the sun rising behind her and the

mountain rising ahead. At last, the weary hills and valleys came to an end. And there was the sea. Gwinna saw for the first time the far thin line where the blue of the sky meets the blue of the sea. There was nothing at all between them, only the mountain, standing alone at the very rim of the world.

It is so far, she thought. How can I ever fly so far? Gliding down along the shore, she heard the cries of the seabirds, "Far! Far! Far!" She heard the sea waves too. Wave upon wave, they roared and sang against the rocks, their foam white as the mountain's ice and snow. Gwinna thought of the song and the harp she hoped to find. "I will go," she said. "No matter how far!"

So she flew out over the shore, leaving all the land she knew behind.

Now and then a gull came to fly with her, or a snow goose, or a graceful tern. Gwinna was glad for the company. But in time, they tilted their wings and flew another way. They had long journeys of their own.

The sun slowly crossed the sky. Gwinna's wings began to ache. The mountain seemed as far as ever, still so far. In all the waves that swelled like hills below, in all the wide blue, Gwinna saw no place to land. She might drop into the sea, too worn out to fly anymore. "No!" she said, trying not to think of it. Instead, she ate the barley cakes, and tried to rest her tired wings on the wind, skimming low over the waves, then up again, the way the seabirds do.

She flew and flew, toward the mountain, hoping to hear the music in the wind. But the winds only carried the cold salt smell of the sea. Sudden shadows blew over the waves, whipping the crests and flinging the spray high into Gwinna's face. These winds roared in her ears. With all her might, Gwinna rode the wild air till she came to gentler winds again, shaken and tossed, but still flying.

By now the sun was not behind her, but before. It was high over the mountain, sending a path of light over the sea. Gwinna hoped with all her heart it was a path for her, leading straight to the mountain. And so it seemed to be. As she flew over the dazzling light, the mountain loomed suddenly near.

It rose right out of the sea, from cliffs of ice at the base, to lofty pinnacles in the sky. Not a breath of wind, nor a single wave, whispered along the cliffs. Around the mountain, a glassy stillness spread over the sea. The water was so clear, Gwinna could see the mountain ice rising up from a blue too deep to know.

Before the great mountain, Gwinna felt smaller than a sparrow, smaller than a wren. How she longed to set her feet down somewhere, and rest. But Grandmother's words came to her. "First, honor the mountain."

As she flew nearer, the cold breath of the mountain came to meet her. It was so still, the cold was gentle to her face, after the wild winds. With slow, quiet strokes, Gwinna began to fly in a circle around the mountain. She didn't know what else a small bird could do to honor such a vast and silent majesty.

She flew by slopes of the purest snow, and sheer ridges of ice. She flew by fissures and caverns, deep and blue as the sea. She flew by frozen waterfalls that seemed to be lit from within. Yet all the way around the mountain, Gwinna heard no singing voice. She saw no green summer leaves, nor any living thing.

I must go to the highest place, she thought, remembering. But her wings were too tired to climb. She glided to a ledge by an icefall. There she sank down in the snow, folding her wings at last, worn out, and hungry.

Reaching into her pockets, Gwinna found not a crumb of barley cake was left. There was only the bit of stone from the mossy crag. And with it, there was a tuft of moss, and in the moss, a tiny white feather.

Gwinna smiled. Tobin, she thought, you did come with me after all. These three things, the stone, the moss and the feather, she set in the ice beside the frozen waterfall. They were all she had from home, to honor the mountain.

Cold water splashed on her hands. Then Gwinna saw that

the icefall was not ice at all, but the clearest water, pouring down the mountainside. She listened for its voice, for the song of falling water. Yet this water made no sound. She was thirsty. She dipped her hands into the silent water, and drank again and again. After that, Gwinna felt as fresh as if she had rested a whole night and a day. Her hunger was gone.

So she spread her wings, and the still breath of the mountain seemed to lift her as she flew, up, and up, and up toward the highest peak.

9

Silence

The peak of the mountain might have been carved of light, it was so radiant. Gwinna stood on the highest crest, with all the mountain beneath her and the sun straight above her head. As far as she could see, on every side, the thin line between the sea and the sky was a single ring, with no beginning and no end.

Gwinna thought, This is the center of the world.

She felt even more like the smallest bird, alone in this high place. No one was there. There was no voice, no leaves, no harp in the wind. The cold of the mountain crept into Gwinna's bones. She shivered, trying to remember Grandmother's words. "Go to the highest place, and sit, and wait, and listen." She thought, Maybe someone will come.

So she found a hollow in the shelter of the crest, and there she sat in the snow. The winds over the sea had torn her feathers ragged. But Gwinna shook them soft again, and wrapped her wings around her as well as she could, like a warm cloak. Underneath, she tucked her dress of fleeces and fur around her legs, and buried her hands in the sleeves.

There she sat, looking out at the sky. The only clouds she saw were the puffs of her own breath.

Gwinna had been in the quiet before, at home when her father and mother sat by the evening fire, and no one spoke. She knew the quiet of mist. And the stillness of stone. She knew the silence of the owls' wings, and her own. But the silence here, on the mountain now, was greater than all of these.

Without a sound, the sun went down over the crest behind her. A rosy glow bloomed in the sky, touching all the mountain's ice and snow with rose. Then, violet shadows crept over the ice, turning to deeper and deeper blue as they went, until they melted into the sky, and everything was dark.

Gwinna shivered and sighed and thought, Oh, Tobin, I wish you were here. Huddled under her wings, she held the memory of Tobin close, to keep her warm.

The silence was even greater in the dark, so deep, so high and vast, it held the mountain, the sea, and the splendor of all the stars. Gwinna sat very still, waiting, listening. She might hear the music of the stars. Yet even the brightest shooting star came and went without a trace of song.

If an hour passed or a whole night, who can say? Time on the mountain is not the same as time anywhere else. If Gwinna slept, her dreams were the same as waking. The silence grew inside her too, as she waited there, with all the stars, like a tiny bird in a nest that has no end.

Slowly, the darkness between the stars began to grow light. As if all the stars were giving themselves away, one to another, all their lights blended into one. Then there was only one silent light, everywhere. Gwinna herself was wrapped in it. She sat as still as if she were part of the mountain. Her cap and her wings were covered with sparkling frost. And then, at last, she heard a whisper of wind in the light.

No, it was the sound of wings. Mighty wings, Gwinna thought, rushing toward the mountain. Someone is coming! All she could see was light, as the wings swept closer and closer. The light grew more and more gold, and the wings seemed to sweep the gold of the light into themselves as they came, until the light took a shape. And Gwinna saw a glorious griffin.

She held her breath, blinking her eyes until it didn't hurt anymore to look at him. He was a beast of light, with the head and breast and wings of an eagle, feathers like flames, and eyes that could see straight into the sun. Gwinna was sure of that.

His two front legs were those of an eagle, with huge talons piercing the snow, as he landed on the mountain peak. His hind legs were those of a lion, and he had a lion's tail.

The griffin folded his mighty wings. He settled himself, as though all the mountain were his home. Fire and sunlight rippled through every feather, and every hair of his fur, to the tip of his noble tail.

Gwinna thought, This is the lord of the mountain. But when she tried to stand, she found her wings were frozen into the snow, and her legs were numb.

The griffin turned to her. His voice was clear as a golden horn. He said her name, "Gwinna."

Gwinna's own voice was only a whisper. She said, "Your Majesty."

Then the griffin raised his head and began to laugh. His laughter rang from the mountaintop, like a bright fanfare of trumpets in the court of a king. He said, "There is no king worthy to rule the center of the world. I am only a guide and a friend to anyone who comes here. You were brave to come. And you have listened well."

"But sir," Gwinna said, "I have heard nothing, no music, no song."

"Silence is before all song," the griffin said. "And you have heard the silence."

Now Gwinna knew it was so. She bowed her head and said softly, "It is greater than the stars."

"Listening has made your ears true," said the griffin. "And one who hears the silence above, may hear the song below." He swished his tail. "I will take you there now, if you wish."

Gwinna said, "Yes, please, I do wish!"

With that, the griffin raised his fiery wings and fanned the air. Gwinna felt a hot wind, melting the ice-frost from her feathers. She stood up, stretched and shook her wings, and made herself ready to fly. Yet the griffin lowered his head. He opened his beak and breathed on the snow before him, until it melted away and the ice beneath it was laid bare. Then he tore through the ice with his talons, to uncover a chasm.

Gwinna shuddered. Before her was a hole that seemed to go down into the mountain forever, into a starless black. She did not want to look down. Her heart was drumming loud and fast.

"I will lead the way," the griffin said. "Do you trust me?"

Gwinna looked across the chasm, into the griffin's eyes. Steady as the sun, his power held her. She was sure he knew the way, be it higher than the mountain, or deeper than the sea.

"Yes," she said. But still she was afraid. Trembling, she pulled her wings in close to her sides.

"That is the way," said the griffin. He pulled his own wings close to him, as an eagle does when he dives. "Now be brave and follow. Keep me in your sight, and you will not be lost."

Then with a bright cry, he plunged down into the hole. Before his light was gone, too fast for thought, Gwinna leaped from the edge, diving straight down after the griffin.

The Tree

Gwinna thought she'd left her heart behind, as she fell after the griffin, faster and faster. The darkness roared in her ears. She heard voices wailing.

"Look, she is falling," they cried.

"She will be hurt. She will be lost."

"Lost forever!"

Gwinna opened her wings to save herself. But the voices whipped the darkness into whirlwinds. They snatched at her dress with invisible hands, spinning her this way and that way. The more she flapped her wings, the worse it was.

In a frenzy, she screamed for the griffin. He was so far down in the chasm, his light was only a star. In a moment more, he would vanish. Keep me in your sight, he had said.

Gwinna cried, "I will not be lost!"

She pulled her wings in tight and dove straight down again. And the cap was torn from her head as she left the voices wailing behind.

Down, and deeper down she went, faster and faster. She held her hands over her heart to keep it with her. The darkness rushed in her face and tore her breath away. But she kept her eyes on the star of the griffin, until he disappeared in a greater light below. Down she fell after him, out of the dark, through drifting clouds in a bright, clear air. She had fallen into the sky of another land.

She spread her wings to slow her fall, swooping down and soaring out over that land, to calm her heart and find her breath again. She saw below her a land she did not know. And yet she felt like a lost child, coming home after a long time.

Wide green hills spread in rings from a meadow in the center, like ripples in a pool. All the land shone as if the drops of the first rain still hung from every leaf. Gwinna saw the glimmer of streams and ponds here and there among the trees. But nowhere did she see any sign of the griffin.

So she glided down to the meadow in the middle of that land. As she folded her wings, the smell of sweet summer grasses came to greet her. Gwinna had never seen any green so green. Every blade of grass was filled with emerald light.

She sat right down and took off her shoes and stockings. The grass was warm and cool at once, gentle to her feet. Then, wherever she stepped in the grass, wildflowers bloomed before her. Gwinna was so happy to see them, she ran from place to place, picking one of every kind and color, just one. Soon she had a glowing bouquet in her hand.

Then she looked up and saw the tree that grew alone in the center of that place. She hadn't stopped to notice it before. The tree was even more radiant than the grass. Gwinna thought the sun itself had come to rest in the cool shade of its leaves. And no wonder. For there, sitting quietly under the tree, was the griffin.

"There you are," Gwinna cried. Her laughter rang out to him like bells. He had been there all the time. The griffin laughed too. And another voice joined in, a pure lilting voice.

As Gwinna came into the shade of the tree, holding out the flowers, the other voice said her name, as if it were part of a song. "Gwinna. At last you have come."

Just a little above her own, Gwinna saw a face smiling at her. There was a glow in the smile, though the face was brown as wood. The eyes were brown too, deep and shining. It was the Tree herself. She was only a girl, like Gwinna, though she was taller.

The Tree wore a gown of velvet moss, all the way to the ground. There were twigs and tiny ferns growing around the Tree's face like a crown. Her arms were not only two, but a hundred and more, reaching up and branching again and again.

Gwinna loved the Tree at once. She felt as if she had always known her. And when the Tree spoke again, Gwinna knew it was her voice she had heard, singing in the wind from the mountain.

The Tree said, "I am happy to see you. No one has come for such a long time. I have been so alone."

Gwinna said softly, "Would you like some flowers?" She wove the flowers from her bouquet into the twigs and ferns around the Tree's face.

"Thank you," said the Tree. "Would you like some berries?"

Looking up, Gwinna saw many fruits hidden there in the leaves. She was hungry. "Thank you," she said, reaching up to pick some for herself, and some for the griffin. The Tree called them berries, yet her fruits were more like pears, red as living rubies, and sweet as plums.

"Please, stay with me and rest," said the Tree. "Stay as long as you like."

"I would like to stay forever," Gwinna said. She felt more at home here with the Tree than anywhere else she had ever been, even her mama and papa's house, even Grandmother's grotto.

The griffin lay down under the Tree, swishing his tail, calm as a lion. Gwinna spread her wings and lay back in the grass beside him. Above them the Tree seemed to fill the sky. Her leaves began to shimmer and shift. Her arms began to sway.

"Ahh," sighed the Tree. "The wind is coming. I will sing you a song."

As Gwinna lay looking up into the leaves, she heard the music of water, of lilting shadows and lights. Every one of the Tree's leaves sang with a voice of its own. She heard them all. They sang like a thousand fluttering birds, all green and joyous, all singing at once. Their many voices rang together as one. And then, Gwinna heard only one voice, the one pure voice of the Tree, singing alone.

She sang the song of the whole world. She sang all the way to her roots. The melody rang deep in the ground where Gwinna lay. It came up again in the grass. And the grasses went on singing in Gwinna's ears, long after the Tree herself was still.

The song rippled out from the Tree, through all the other grasses and trees of that land, farther and farther away, until everything was still. And no one spoke. For silence is before all song, and after.

But only for a time. Soon the birds awoke in the hills. Doves began to coo. Crickets began to chirp. And bees began to hum over the meadow.

The Tree's Gift

The griffin sat up, shook his fiery feathers, and began to preen them with his beak.

Gwinna lay a while more. She felt she was floating in the grass. Now she had heard the song she came so far to hear. She was sure it stirred even the stones in the ground and gave them joy. Yet, there was still a wish in Gwinna's heart, waiting to be told. It burned like a secret flame.

She sat up, and ran her fingers lightly over the grass, as if to play a tune there. "How do you make such a beautiful song?" she asked the Tree.

"It is the wind's song too," said the Tree. "See, now the wind is gone, and my leaves are still. I cannot sing alone."

Gwinna said, "Will the wind come again?"

"Oh yes," said the Tree. "The wind is swift and free, it comes and goes, and it always comes again. Alone the wind is silent, you see. Even the wind cannot sing alone."

Gwinna's green eyes were suddenly bright. "I do see," she said. "The wind plays your leaves. The wind comes and plays you. Like a harp!"

"Yes," said the Tree, her face aglow under the crown of wildflowers. "When the wind comes to me, that is the happiest thing I know. If I could not sing, I think I would die. And so I sing."

"Even when there is no one to hear?"

"Yes," said the Tree.

Gwinna looked down at her hands. "If only I could be like you," she said. "When the wind comes to me, it has no leaves to play. My feathers do not sing. But I hear the music in the wind, I do. Sometimes, the wind blows your song to me, far over the sea. It is too big to hold and too beautiful to keep. But I don't know how to give it to anyone."

She thought of Grandmother, wrapped in her shawl. She thought of Tobin, and all her dear brothers and sisters, the animals. She thought of her mama and papa, who could not hear. Tears sprang into Gwinna's eyes. She tried to blink them away. "I wish," she stammered, "I, I wish . . ."

Then the pure, lilting voice of the Tree and the golden voice of the griffin spoke together. "What do you wish?"

"I wish for a harp," Gwinna said at last. "A harp of my own.

A harp for the wind to play. Oh please tell me what I must do. I will give anything."

Gwinna didn't mean to cry, especially in front of the griffin. But she could not help it. All the wishing inside her came spilling out of her eyes. The salty tears ran down her face and dripped into the grass. They sank into the ground, and there the Tree tasted the tears in her roots.

"Ohh," sighed the Tree.

Gwinna sniffled and rubbed her face on her sleeve.

After a time, the Tree said softly, "I have a wish too. I wish to give you something, Gwinna, something of my own. Will you please accept my gift?"

Gwinna didn't know what the Tree could mean. But she looked up, and nodded, and said, "Yes."

Then the Tree's face was lit with such a happiness, all her leaves turned from green to gold. The leaves fluttered, bright as flames, and then they left the Tree as if they could fly. It was the wind who came again and whisked the leaves away. Gwinna heard them singing as they swirled up into the sky, scattering everywhere over that wide green land.

"You've lost your leaves!" Gwinna cried.

The Tree only smiled. "I gladly give them all away for a friend."

Now, all the Tree's arms were bare. Even her gown of velvet moss was gone, and the Tree wore only bark. Her face was rutted and wrinkled. But her eyes still shone.

Then the Tree said to the griffin, "Will you please give me to Gwinna now?"

The griffin bowed to the Tree, as he would to a queen. And before he raised himself again, he was changed. The feathers fell from his head. All his fiery sunlight rippled into another shape. And Gwinna saw, in place of the griffin, an old man bowing to the Tree. His beard was white as a hundred winter snows. Yet when the old man stood up, he was straight and strong. His brow was stern as an eagle's. He had the griffin's eyes.

The old man rolled up his sleeves. Then he lifted an ax with a golden blade.

Gwinna shouted, "No!"

But the sound never came out of her mouth. For she had already said, "Yes."

"Gwinna," said the Tree, "Grandfather Griffin does this only because I ask him to. Don't be afraid."

But as Gwinna saw the ax swing and the blade flash, she could not bear to look. She ran from the Tree and covered her face with her wings. Still, she heard every Chop! Chop! Chop!

And she felt every blow ring through her as it rang through the trunk of the Tree. Chop! Chop!

Gwinna trembled and shook, all the way through her feet and into the ground, as if she had roots where she stood. Chop! Chop! Just when she could not bear anymore, the Tree cried out. With a loud crack, she fell. And Gwinna fell too.

I 2

Grandfather Griffin

How long she lay there who can say? Gwinna was neither dead nor asleep. She had no memories, no dreams. Her wings, her arms and legs might be in pieces all over the meadow, for all she knew. She felt nothing.

The old man came and lifted her in his arms. He carried her along a stream that ran over the meadow to a hollow where the stream had made a pool. The pool was lined with the greenest grasses. Here and there under the clear water, wildflowers shone like jewels.

He laid Gwinna down in the pool and said, "Bathe here now. The water will refresh you." Then he went away.

Gwinna listened to the stream spilling into the pool. "All is new, and all, and all is new," it seemed to say. Her old brown dress slowly melted away in the clear water. Gwinna lay as bare as when she was born. Feeling came back to her arms and legs and wings. She wiggled her fingers and toes. The water swirled around her, and the grasses under the water washed her like gentle hands.

When Gwinna stepped out of the pool, she felt whole and fresh and new. She shook her wings, and dried herself in the warm air. There was no sun overhead, but Gwinna had her memory again. I am deep inside the mountain, she thought, in the land of the Tree. But how empty the meadow was now. The Tree was gone.

Spread in the grass beside the pool, Gwinna saw a long green gown. "The Tree's dress." She sank to her knees and touched the velvet, soft as silken moss. There were two openings in the back, just right for Gwinna's wings. "Oh," she whispered, "my friend. Why did you give me your only dress? Now you are gone. I will never see you again."

Yet when Gwinna pulled the dress on, a peacefulness came over her, as if she wore the Tree's own shade. She must have grown a little taller too, for the long green dress fit her perfectly.

Then Gwinna followed the stream back across the meadow. The grasses smelled as sweet as before, and the bees were still humming. Slowing to a trickle, the little stream led her back to the place of the Tree. Now there was only a stump. And Gwinna saw the clear water bubbling up in that very place, from the Tree's roots.

The old man had cut the fallen tree into pieces. He had set up a workbench, and now he was taking tools from a large wooden box. Gwinna saw a spokeshave, a mallet and chisels. She had seen such tools before, in her papa's shed.

"Are you a woodworker, sir?" she asked.

"Yes," said the old man. "I am a master."

Gwinna asked him, "What are you going to make?"

"I shall make a harp," he said. "And you shall help me. For the hands that play this harp must help to build it."

Then Gwinna nearly flew away with joy. Her feet left the ground. She threw her arms around the old man's neck, and kissed him on the cheek. Under his stern brow, his eyes were full of sunlight. Smiling, he patted her gently back down to the ground. "Now then," he said, "shall we begin?"

Grandfather Griffin taught her many things. He showed her all the wood from the Tree. His hands knew the grain in every part. "The true voice of a harp is in the wood," he said.

Gwinna was surprised. "Not in the strings?"

"Oh there must be strings," he said. "But without the wood, the strings are nothing. They are like words on the tongue that do not ring from deep inside the heart." He smiled. "The heart of this wood will sing like no other."

Gwinna knelt in the grass. She touched the wood, the

pieces chosen for her harp. "The Tree has given me more than I knew."

"Yes," said Grandfather Griffin softly.

He gave her an old work apron to tie over the velvet dress. Then he showed her the use of his tools and what to do. Before long, chips and shavings of wood were caught in Gwinna's coppery hair, and scattered around her feet, as she began to hollow the wood for the soundbox.

But only Grandfather Griffin's hands knew how to finish the carving, so the wood was strong where it must be strong, and fine where it must be fine, never too thick or too thin. Then Gwinna helped him shape and smooth the pillar for the harp, and the graceful curving neck. Together, they fitted the neck and the pillar, and joined them well with the soundbox.

"A harp must be very strong," Grandfather told her.

"Graceful and strong," Gwinna mused, "like a tree."

While they worked, Grandfather Griffin whistled, and Gwinna hummed to herself. When they were hungry, they ate some ruby fruits, saved from the Tree and kept in a wooden bowl. When they were thirsty, they followed the last trickle of the stream to the pool of clear water, to drink.

Gwinna watched while Grandfather Griffin made two rows of holes in the harp, one in the soundbox for the strings, and one in the neck for the tuning pins. When he was done, he laid his hand on Gwinna's shoulder. "Now, you must make a design of your own in the harp," he said. He brought out his finest carving tools, and then he lay down to rest.

Gwinna knew the ways of the wood and the tools by now, but she hoped she wouldn't ruin the harp with a slip of her hand. She thought and thought. She drew with Grandfather's pencil on scraps of wood, until she knew the lines and shapes she wanted. Then she set to carving, all by herself. Her hand did slip, more than once. She nicked her fingers with the sharp chisels, and stopped the bleeding on her apron. Then she worked on, with even more care, as slowly as she knew Grandfather Griffin would. She did her very best. And then, with a clean cloth, she rubbed all the wood of the harp until it shone.

"Ahhh," said Grandfather Griffin, when he saw it. "You have honored me. And you have honored the Tree."

In the head of the harp, Gwinna had carved a griffin. And along the soundbox and up the pillar, she had carved delicate branches and leaves.

"My harp," she said, "my own true harp. Oh Grandfather, it is all I have wished for. It is more than I ever dreamed!"

They admired the harp together. Every part was in harmony with every other part. Nothing was too big or too small.

The harp was exactly right for Gwinna to hold in her arms, in her own lap.

"Grandfather," she asked, "where are the strings?"

Grandfather Griffin was smiling, stroking his long beard. "They are here," he said. "You must pull them from my beard. The long hairs will have the lowest notes, and the short hairs will have the highest."

So one by one, Gwinna pulled the snow-white hairs from Grandfather Griffin's beard. Then, one by one, he strung the hairs on the harp. He tied each one below, and with a golden tuning key he turned each tuning pin above, till all the hairs were stretched so fine, Gwinna wondered if they would break. He did not pluck the strings, but holding his ear close to the harp, Grandfather Griffin seemed to hear every one. When he was satisfied at last, his face shone like the sun.

Gwinna reached out for the harp, to touch the strings, to hear the wood sing. But Grandfather Griffin caught her hand in his own. "No," he said. "There is one thing more to do. It is the greatest thing of all. And you alone can do it."

13

Wood, Fire, and Gold

First, he gathered the wood that was left from the Tree. Gwinna helped him to lay it around the stump. Then, bending down on his knees, Grandfather Griffin breathed on the wood until it began to glow. Flames sprang up and danced around the stump, sun-bright and hot. Yet, how strange. The wood gave itself to the flames without a sound. The fire was silent.

Gwinna asked, "Grandfather, what is the thing I must do?"

Grandfather Griffin brought the harp and placed it in her hands. Then, pointing into the heart of the fire, where the stump of the Tree was glowing red, he said to Gwinna, "Set the harp there."

Gwinna looked at him in horror. Her face burned. The grass was too warm under her feet. She held the harp closer to her and stepped away from the fire. Then she turned and half ran, half flew to the far end of the meadow.

There the grass was cool. She sank down in the shadows, rocking the harp in her lap, and whispering, "No, no, I will never put you in the fire. I will keep you safe."

She wanted to play a sweet, comforting tune. And so, she touched a string. With a snap, the string broke. Gwinna gasped. She touched another string. It snapped too. And a third. No sweet tune rang in the harp's wood.

Gwinna sat as still as a stone. She didn't know what to do. Her thoughts whirled. I will fly away! I will take my harp to another place! But she did not go.

She saw the fire rising where the Tree had been, in the center of the meadow. It was so bright, everything else seemed dark, even the sky. Sparks swirled up from the flames, just as the golden leaves of the Tree had swirled up in the wind.

Her own words came back to her. "I will give anything." But it was the Tree who gave. She had given everything. Gwinna thought, She gave her life to be this harp for me. Even now, as Gwinna touched the wood, she knew it was the Tree she held in her arms, and the Tree's life still, not her own. "I have only shaped your wood a little," she whispered to the harp. "You are all I love and all I have hoped for. Oh please, please tell me what you wish."

She sat very still, listening. Then, she heard a whisper in the harp's wood, as of a breath among leaves, a faint, lilting whisper. "If you love me, give me to the fire, that I may sing."

Gwinna held her breath, hoping to hear other words. But her ears had heard true. The harp said nothing more. She reached up, and pulled three coppery hairs from her own head. Then she strung the hairs on the harp, just as she had seen Grandfather Griffin do. She would not give her harp to the fire with broken strings. Then, walking slowly through the grass, she carried the harp back across the meadow.

Grandfather Griffin stood by the fire, waiting quietly. Without a word, Gwinna stepped closer to the flames. Her hands trembling, she reached into the fire and set the harp upon the glowing stump. She wanted to cry out. But the Tree's wood was brave and silent as it burned. Gwinna held her cry between her teeth as she pulled her hands out of the searing flames.

She backed away, yet she felt she was standing in the fire herself. Her hands burned. The heat raged up through her arms and all through her. She saw the fire leap and dance around the harp, and she felt her own heart bursting into flames. A hundred fingers of fire played the harp, but the harp did not cry out. Its wood turned to red, to gold, then to a blazing light. And Gwinna could see the harp no more, for the harp and the fire were one.

Then, through the tears that burned in her eyes, Gwinna saw the face of the Tree in the fire. She saw the Tree's arms, dancing and swaying. Her leaves were all shimmering flames, singing her last song, a song with no sound, a song of heat and light.

The light rose up from the fire and filled the sky. And suddenly, Gwinna felt a great sweetness. All the pain was burned away. Her friend was free.

She looked at her hands. They were glowing. Every trace of a nick or a cut was gone. Her hands were as clean as if she had washed them in purest water.

Nothing was left of the fire now, only a fine blue smoke curling up from a ring of ashes. There in the smoke, like a vision in the midst of the ashes, Gwinna saw the stump. It was burned yet it was not burned. And there, like a vision upon the stump, was the harp.

Gwinna took a step closer. She could hardly believe her eyes. The soundbox, the pillar and graceful neck were there. The griffin she had carved was there, and the fine branches and leaves. Even the strings were there, every one. But now, all the harp was made of dazzling light.

Beside her, she heard Grandfather Griffin say, "Nothing true is lost. The fire only makes it pure and strong." Before Gwinna could touch the harp of light, he said, "Let it cool."

As the harp cooled, the light turned to solid gold. And as the gold cooled, the harp turned to rich, brown wood once more. The fire had polished the wood to a noble shine. The strings were gold, as if they were never hairs at all, but pulled from the sun.

Grandfather Griffin took Gwinna's hands, and held them gently and said, "You also are strong and true. You have given everything. You gave all you love to the fire. And now, the harp is your own."

Gwinna had no words. The old man knew, and he smiled tenderly. Then he gave her the golden tuning key, to keep in her pocket, always.

"Will you teach me to play?" Gwinna asked.

"No," said Grandfather Griffin, "I am only a woodworker. It is the wind who will teach you to play. Come and sit, here in the place of the Tree."

He lifted the harp from the stump. Gwinna untied the work apron she wore. When she stepped through the ring of ashes, and sat upon the stump, she felt as a princess feels, coming to her throne for the first time. Lights from the fire still shone in her coppery hair. Splendid new feathers had grown in place of the old. But Gwinna hardly knew it, as she folded her wings behind her, and smoothed the green velvet dress over her lap.

Grandfather Griffin gave the harp to her. The wood was

warm in her hands. Gwinna set the harp between her knees, and pulled it back to rest at her shoulder. When she looked up, her eyes were clear as sunlight in green water.

Then, Grandfather Griffin said,

"Fingers of light, fingers of wind,
Let the song of the harp begin."

And the wind came.

14

The Harp

The wind came, circling the place of the Tree. It ruffled the feathers of Gwinna's wings. It touched the strings of her harp. They quivered and shone, and sweet murmurs rang in the harp's wood.

Gwinna followed the wind's touch with her fingers. Where a string shimmered, she plucked. She plucked, and the harp rang out. And so the wind showed her the ways of all the strings. She felt each one against her fingertip, still warm with fire. She heard each one, each with a tone of its own. The whole harp rang, with every string she touched, pure as a bell of gold with many tones. And Gwinna felt the wood of the harp ringing where it touched her shoulder and her knees.

The wind taught her to play, simple tunes and simple airs, gay, tender and free. Gwinna's fingers stumbled to follow. Yet every note was sweet to hear, for the voice of the harp was true as the voice of the Tree. Gwinna felt the sound of the harp ringing through her, through her arms, her lap, down into the stump. Soon her fingers were light as leaves and quick as running water, dancing on the strings. She and her harp were one. She sat on the stump like a bird lost in its song. And she saw nothing else around her.

She did not see Grandfather Griffin sitting down in the grass. She did not see his face, shining and changing as he listened. She didn't see in him the face of a young man, not much older than herself, a princely young man who gazed at her, enchanted. She did not see the feathers grow like a robe of sunlight upon him, and the wings and the tail and the talons, until he was a noble griffin again.

She saw only the light of the strings where her fingers danced with the wind. She did not see the shoot of green that grew up from the roots of the stump, up through the ashes. Up and up it grew behind her, swaying with the music of her harp, growing taller and reaching out with arms: not only two, but a hundred and more, branching again and again. She did not see the radiant buds everywhere above her. She did not see the many petals unfolding.

Then, with the last notes of its song, the wind swirled up from the harp and stirred the tree. Gwinna heard the sound of a thousand sighs. A fragrance showered down around her, and Gwinna breathed it in. Only then did she look up from the

harp. Then she saw the griffin lying in the grass at her feet, and the cloud of white blossoms over her head.

"Can it be?" Gwinna whispered. Turning, she saw the face of the Tree, smiling down at her.

"Ahh," sighed the Tree. "I felt a song of the wind just now, all the way to my roots. I felt a song, and I could not stay below anymore. See, I am here, I am new."

Already, the Tree wore a new gown of moss. There were new twigs and ferns, and snowy blossoms around her face. Her brown cheeks were smooth, as before. Gwinna looked up into the Tree's eyes. She was the same Tree. Yet now she was more than a girl.

"It is you," Gwinna said, gazing up in wonder. "You are taller now, and even more beautiful."

White petals drifted down into Gwinna's hair. "So are you," said the Tree.

Lifting her harp, Gwinna stood and opened her wings in joy. "O sister Tree," she said, "see what a gift you have given me. Now I sing the songs of the wind, with my own hands." There was a new lilt in her voice. She felt a tingling in her wings. She could hardly keep her feet on the ground. "Now I can give the songs of the wind to everyone I love, my brothers and sisters, Grandmother and . . ."

She stopped. How long have I been away, she wondered,

how long? A year, or only a day? Gwinna did not know. It might have been forever.

The green meadow was home to her now. She turned to the griffin, who sat like living sunlight there in the grass. She turned to the blossoming Tree. She didn't want to leave this place, nor these two friends.

"I want to stay with you and never leave," she said to them. "But I must go. I made a promise. I hope I'm not too late."

"Gwinna," said the griffin, "now you are free to come and go, like the wind."

She set her harp on the stump for a moment, under the Tree. Then she went to the griffin and put her arms around his neck, pressing her cheek to his breast. Under the feathers, she heard the deep drum of the griffin's heart. "I hope you will come to the mountain again someday," he said. "You are dearer to me than you can know. And I am here, always."

Gwinna thought she saw a tear in the griffin's eye. As he rose up on his lion's legs, the tear fell to her brow like a kiss. Spreading his mighty wings, with a swish of his tail, the griffin flew up into the sky, higher and higher, until he vanished into the light, just as he had come.

A sigh passed through the Tree. "I, too, am always here," she said. "Here is where I have always been, and where I shall always be."

Gwinna asked her, "Will you be lonely?"

"No," said the Tree, "now I will never be alone." Her blossoms stirred. "Though my roots are here, I will go with you, for I am with you in the harp. See what a gift you have given me. Now, I too shall fly! And wherever you go, when you play the songs of the wind, I too will sing."

Gwinna kissed the Tree's smooth brown cheek. "I will carry you with me, always," she whispered. And there was no need to say the word good-bye.

She took her harp in her arms, and stepping out from under the Tree, she raised her wings and flew up over the meadow. Below, the white flowering Tree seemed to grow smaller and smaller. Three white doves flew up from the hills around the meadow, bringing the scent of blossoms in their wings. They flew with Gwinna up through the clouds, until the sky grew dark. "Coo-ooo," they said, "coo-ooo." Then the doves returned to the wide green land below.

Gwinna flew on, up and up. The sky grew darker and more and more narrow, until it was all black. The only light was far above, like a star. As Gwinna flew toward it, she heard voices wailing, as before.

"Play a song for us."

"We will give you a castle. We will give you a crown."

"We will tell your name to the world."

"Give us a song!"

Gwinna did not listen. Quiet as an owl, she flew up through the darkness, past the voices, holding the harp before her. And she did not touch a single string, as she flew up through the chasm, toward the light of the opening, high in the mountain.

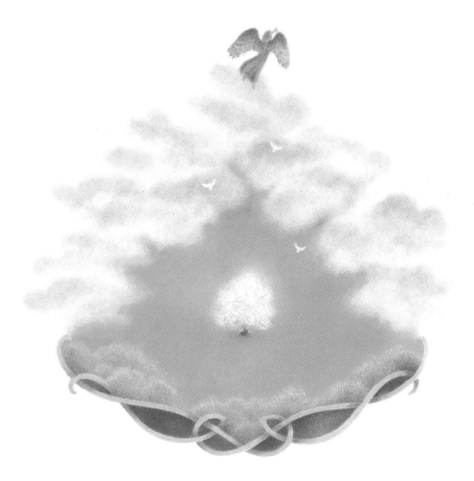

15

A Year and a Day

Once again, Gwinna stood on the highest crest of the mountain. The ice was so cold, it stung her feet. But she smiled to think of her shoes, left in the green grass below, forgotten. No matter the cold, the sun was high above her head. All the sky was blue.

This is the center of the world, she thought. From this place, I can go anywhere. Every way she looked, the ring of the sea and the sky was the same, with no beginning and no end. She could not tell which way she had come, or which way to go.

Lifting her harp, she called out to the wind. "O wind, please come and play in my harp, so I may know my way."

Then, four winds blew, each from a different way. Gwinna turned, to hear each one in the harp. One wind hummed in the highest strings. Another wind played up and down, merry laughing sounds. A third wind whispered of castles and crowns. The last wind played in the lowest strings, murmuring, "Huuu, huuuu."

Gwinna knew then which way to go. Spreading her wings, she soared slowly once, twice, three times around the mountain peak, to honor the great silence of the mountain, and all the mountain had given. Then she flew out over the sea, holding the harp before her.

She flew and flew, riding the air like a seabird over the waves. Playful sea winds came and went, lifting the spray from the waves to touch her feet. Gwinna held the harp steady, listening to the winds in the strings, learning the songs of the sea by heart as she flew.

Then at last, she came to the sea's end, where the gulls cried and the waves rushed to the shore. She did not stop to rest, but flew on and on, toward the hills and valleys of home. But oh what a sad lament the wind played in her harp as she flew. The strings shivered. The wood of the harp rang with sighs. All the land below lay in a wintry sleep, like an old, old woman too weary to wake again. There was not even a blanket of snow to keep her warm, only white ribbons of ice, the frozen rivers and streams. A thin gray mist lay over the hills like a tattered shawl.

Grandmother must be sleeping too, at home in the grotto, Gwinna thought, with the animals and Tobin. I hope they are keeping warm. She flew on a little faster. Her wings were strong and silent. But the chill of the land swept over her face, her feet, her hands.

The sun went down behind the mountain, far away. Dark shadows of dusk drew over the empty fields below, over a winding road, over a village. But Gwinna saw no smoke curling up from the chimneys. She heard no clatter of pots and pans in the streets. Nor did she hear any owls calling from the trees. Over the dreary woodlands she flew, over the dark forest, until at last she came to the old meadow. She glided down to land by the crag, and the frozen leaves on the frozen grass crumbled under her feet. Winter has been here too long, she thought, too long.

She hurried into the forest, through black columns of trees. She could see as well as an owl. She came to the grotto and pushed the ivy curtain aside, calling, "Grandmother, are you awake? I am here!"

There was no glimmer of silver light in the grotto. It smelled dimly of leafmold still, but the water that once trickled from the stone was frozen. There wasn't a sound. Gwinna looked all around in the darkness. Grandmother was not there. And there were no wolf puppies, no brother bear, no fox, no rabbits, no deer.

Slowly Gwinna set her harp down in Grandmother's empty

chair. Then, on an old root by the bed, she saw one small pale shape. "Tobin!" One eye blinked open, then another, two gold moons, midnight in the center. Gwinna wanted to laugh and cry at once. "Tobin. You're here."

He bobbed his head and shook his wings and flew to Gwinna's arm. "Hu. Hu. Huu."

"Oh Tobin," she said, stroking his soft feathers. "I'm so happy to see you. But where is Grandmother? Where are all the others?"

Tobin walked up and down Gwinna's arm, hooting, "Hu! Hu! Hu-huuuu!" Slowly then, drowsily, the other owls appeared in the branches above. When they saw Gwinna standing there, they flew down into the grotto.

"We have missed you. Oooo, tu-whooo. We thought you forgot us. We thought you were lost. It has been so cold, so long."

Gwinna asked them, "How long?"

"A year and a day," said the great gray owl, "whoo-OOOO."

Gwinna held her hand over her heart. Her voice trembled. "Where is Grandmother? Tell me. Is she with the stones?"

The owls only answered, "Huuu, huuuu."

"Where," Gwinna asked them, "where?"

"We don't know," said the owls sadly, "we don't know."

Their voices rang with a low thrumming sound in the strings of the harp.

Whirling around, Gwinna took her harp and said to the owls, "Come with me. All of you, come! We are going to look for her."

So the owls roused themselves. They flew with Gwinna, out over the forest, into the moonless night. Tobin flew close beside her. The owls called and called. Gwinna looked and looked. But nowhere in all the forest did she find any faint silver glow.

At last they came to a hillside, where there was a house of stone. "Grandmother!" Gwinna called. "Grandmother, are you there?"

The owls flew to the chimney, the stone gables and eaves. Gwinna set her feet on the frozen ground. "I know this house," she whispered. The stone door was neither open nor closed. Mist hung in the doorway. A cold shadow crept into Gwinna's heart.

"Mama? Papa?"

No one answered. Slowly, Gwinna folded her wings. Holding her harp close, she stepped inside the house. Tobin followed.

The house was dark as the night outside, and just as cold. In the darkness, Gwinna could see the floor, the table, the bread on the table, even the wood in the hearth, all of stone. Tobin flew through the house, looking for Grandmother. She was not there. But Gwinna saw two figures, wrapped in ribbons of mist.

She set her harp on the table. Then she began to brush the air with her wings, sweeping the mist away and out the door. When the last shreds of mist were gone, there was a man standing, and a woman beside him in her chair. They were still as two statues. Tobin perched on the man's head, but he did not stir.

Gwinna touched the cold stone of his sleeve. "Papa, I am here," she said. She kissed the woman's fine carved hair. "Mama, I am here."

Only silence greeted her. Their eyes were closed, their hands pressed to their ears. All was just as it was the day the owls came for her, so long ago.

Tobin flew to perch on the mantle shelf. He closed his wings and watched. Gwinna stood listening to the silence. There in the corners, under a stair, behind a cupboard door, she heard the last dim echoes of her mama's and papa's words. "Do not listen, do not look. Be as still as a stone. Don't be afraid, we will never let you go."

"But I have gone," Gwinna said. "And I have come back again."

There was no reply. Their own words had cast the spell that bound them in the sleep of stone. Gwinna knew they might never wake again. She looked at her mama and papa in sorrow. Her heart was too heavy even for tears.

"Oh Tobin," she sighed, "what can I do?" She sank down on the stool her papa had made for her. How small it seemed. Yet somehow, as she sat there, she thought of the stump of the Tree.

She took her harp into her lap. The wood was chilled. She began to rub it warm with the hem of her velvet dress. And Gwinna knew that within the wood was gold, and within the gold was light, and within the light was a voice, pure and true.

Before all song is silence, she thought. Even the silence of stone.

She took the golden tuning key from her pocket, and carefully tuned every string. Then, Gwinna said to the statues, "Mama, Papa, even if you never see me, and even if you never hear, I will play my harp for you. I will give you the song from the mountain."

16

The Song

The golden strings shone in the dark, as Gwinna began to play. A song flowed from her harp. The song washed against the walls like sea waves. It danced around the statues like a wind. It fluttered through the house like birds, singing the tunes of many leaves.

Gwinna's hands glowed. Her fingers danced on the strings, bright as fire, and the harp sang out with the one pure voice of the Tree. Her song rose from the harp and filled the house with light. And cold gray shadows passed from the walls.

Tapping, tapping her bare foot on the floor, Gwinna played with a touch so light, every note fell as a drop of golden rain. The rain of light fell everywhere, on everything in the house. It drenched the table, the floor, the chairs. It soaked into the stone. It poured down on the head of the man and the woman, over their faces, over their hands. It filled the stone apron in the woman's lap and overflowed. It dripped down on the man's stone working shoes. Then, softly, so softly it seemed to be

part of the song itself, the man's foot began to tap on the floor. Under her skirt, the woman's foot was tapping, tapping too.

The door swung open, simple wood again. Flames leaped up from the wood in the fireplace. The song poured down through the wooden planks in the floor and rippled out through the walls. Then at last, when Gwinna's hands were still and she looked up from the harp, she saw the man lifting the woman from her chair as if to dance. Echoes of song still rang in the room. Gwinna's mama and papa were smiling. Their cheeks were rosy, their eyes open wide.

Turning, they looked at her in surprise. "Who are you?"

Gwinna was so surprised herself, she could hardly speak. "Mama, Papa!"

Then they knew her. "Gwinna," they said, "our girl!" She set her harp aside and stood to greet them.

"But you are more than a girl," they said. "How can it be? Only a moment ago, we closed our eyes . . ."

"No, Mama, no, Papa," Gwinna said. "It has been a long time." She kissed her mother's soft, warm cheek, and she hugged her father, tears of joy streaming down her face.

Gwinna's mother touched the feathers of her wings. "How beautiful they are," she said. And she touched the green velvet of her dress.

Gwinna's father touched the harp. His woodworker's hand

traced every curve, the delicate lines, and the griffin. "This is finely made," he said. "The work of a master."

"Hu! Hu!" A small white owl flew from the mantle to perch on Gwinna's arm. She lifted him up. "This is Tobin," she said.

Just then, there was a knock at the door, though the door was open. Gwinna's mother went to see who it was. She made a deep curtsy in the doorway. "Mother of the Owls," she said. "If you have come for your child, see, she is here."

"O foolish woman," said a voice outside, "it is too late to keep your promise. But raise yourself now. All is well."

Then Gwinna's mother said, "Please do come in."

It might have been the moon herself, coming in the door, the silver light that filled the house was so great. It was only an old woman, wearing a shawl of feathers. Gwinna ran to the old woman's arms.

"Grandmother! Where have you been?"

"Huuuu," said the old woman. A thousand wrinkles gathered around her smile. "I have been across the sea. I have been to the mountain. I have been to the Tree. There I tasted her ruby fruits, and rested in her shade. I have been in a holy fire. And I have come back again."

Gwinna said, "Grandmother, how have you been everywhere I have been? You have seen all that I have seen."

"In the wind of a song I have been there, in the light of a

song I have seen," Grandmother said. "As I lay in my bed below this place, deep down in the dark, I heard a voice singing. Oh she sang of many things, and her song came pouring down to touch me. So I awoke. I followed that voice. And here I am."

Gwinna laid her hand on the harp. "It was the voice of the Tree who woke you," she said.

"Yes," Grandmother nodded. "Yet a harp can never sing alone. Your hands have given her song to me. I thank you, my Gwinna. For still I am old, older than anyone knows. But now, I have heard the song from the heart of the world once more. And I am new."

With that, the Mother of the Owls opened her shawl. And there within it, Gwinna saw all the hills and valleys. She saw the gray mists lifting away. She heard the rivers and streams flowing. She heard the song of her harp ringing in all the land, in new grasses springing up, and tender buds unfolding. The forest, the fields, and all the woodlands turned to radiant green. Gwinna saw that Grandmother too was growing, taller and taller. Soon she was greater than the house. Her shawl spread far as the sea, and farther, wide as wings holding the sky. The drum of her heart beat softly everywhere. She had grown so tall and great, her face was high above, where the moon should be. Above her still were the stars.

"O Grandmother," Gwinna said, looking up into her face, "you are above and below. You hold all the world in your arms. Mother of everyone."

"Hoo, h-hoo-HOOO," called the owls from the rooftop. Gwinna found she was standing outside the house. Tobin was on her shoulder, her father and mother beside her, though none of them knew just when they had come through the door.

"Look," said Gwinna's mother. Every blade of grass was filled with emerald light. Wildflowers of every color were blooming at her feet, and all around the well.

"Look," said Gwinna's father, pointing far beyond the end of the valley. There was the mountain.

But Gwinna wasn't looking at the mountain. There were swallows swooping over her head, and crows flapping over the trees, and sparrows and wrens flitting from bush to bush. Foxes and rabbits came out from under the thickets. A stag and a doe stepped out from between the trees. Then came a wolf with three young wolves, full-grown. They ran to Gwinna, wagging their tails and licking her hands and face. A hummingbird whizzed by: "Zeee!" And a bear came lumbering up the hill.

All the while, the village bells rang in the valley below. The sounds of children's laughter skipped up the hillside. Soon the village children appeared, running in their bare feet.

When they saw the girl with the great wings, her green eyes

and coppery hair, when they saw the wolves, the bear, foxes, rabbits and deer all around her, the children from the village were shy. They whispered, "Is it Gwinna?"

When Gwinna saw them, she was shy for a moment too. Then she said, "Here are my brothers and sisters. Come and meet them." So the children and the animals came to meet one another. And all the children wanted to see the tiny white owl, whose name was Tobin.

Then Gwinna felt a new joy. It grew inside her like a tree, too big to hold and too beautiful to keep. She ran and brought her harp to the hillside. There she sat in the grass, with all her brothers and sisters gathered around. Just as she set the harp in her lap, rocking it back to her shoulder, a warm wind stirred the wildflowers. The wind played in the children's hair and ruffled the animals' fur. Gwinna smiled. Then, she lifted her hands to the shining strings.

There is Gwinna's story. No one has ever told me the end, but this much more I know.

She pulled a feather from her wing and said, "My dear Mama and Papa, I must go. But I will come again. And if you ever need me, hold my feather up to the wind, and I shall come to you."

Moon after moon, summer, fall, winter and spring, Gwinna flew through all the land and many lands beyond. The owls often flew with her at night, and Tobin was always with her.

Gwinna carried her harp wherever she went, to castles and cottages, barns and mansions and huts. She played her harp by the firesides, by sickbeds, cradles and thrones. No song she played was quite like any other, for Gwinna's songs were the wind's songs too, and the wind is never the same.

In the villages, at dusk, there were still a few who went out in the streets to beat upon pots and pans. "Beware!" they cried. "She who flies with the owls is a witch."

But Gwinna did not go where the doors were closed to her. Many others opened wide, for the people knew the voice of her harp would fill the smallest hut with joy, and ease the deepest sorrow.

In that land, they say that Gwinna comes and goes, even to this day. Though her wings are silent, quiet as the clouds, they say if you sit and wait and listen, you may hear her harp in the light, in the leaves, in the wind.